PUSH! DIG! SCOOP!

A Construction Counting Rhyme

Rhonda Gowler Greene

illustrated by **Daniel Kirk**

BLOOMSBURY

LONDON OXFORD NEW YORK NEW DELHI SYDNEY

Bloomsbury Publishing, London, Oxford, New York, New Delhi and Sydney

First published in the United States of America in 2016
by Bloomsbury Children's Books
1385 Broadway, New York, New York 10018

This edition first published in Great Britain in 2016 by Bloomsbury Publishing Plc
50 Bedford Square, London WC1B 3DP

www.bloomsbury.com

BLOOMSBURY is a registered trademark of Bloomsbury Publishing Plc

Text copyright © Rhonda Gowler Greene 2016
Illustrations copyright © Daniel Kirk 2016

The moral rights of the author and illustrator have been asserted

A CIP catalogue record for this book is available from the British Library

ISBN 978 1 4088 8166 8

All papers used by Bloomsbury Publishing are natural, recyclable products made
from wood grown in well managed forests. The manufacturing processes
conform to the environmental regulations of the country of origin

Printed in China by Leo Paper Products, Heshan, Guangdong

1 3 5 7 9 10 8 6 4 2

For my book buddies,
Julian, Mackenzie and Baby Bossory. We "dig" books!
— R.G.G.

For Ethan
— D.K.

Over by the dirt pile in the sizzling summer sun
works a mummy bulldozer with her little dozer **ONE**.

"Push!" says the mummy. "I push!" says the one.
So they push oosh oosh in the sizzling summer sun.

Over by the dirt pile — what a tough and burly crew! —
works a great big daddy digger with his little diggers **TWO**.

"Dig!" says the daddy. "We dig!" say the two.
So they dig *schlup* schlup. What a tough and burly crew!

Over by the dirt pile, just as mighty as can be,
works a daddy wheel loader with his little loaders **THREE**.

"Scoop!" says the daddy. "We scoop!" say the three.
So they scoop sloop sloop, just as mighty as can be.

Over by the dirt pile, tipping loads all set to pour,
works a mummy dumper truck with her little dumpers **FOUR**.

"Spill!" says the mummy. "We spill!" say the four.
So they spill plomp plomp. Now they're ready for some more!

Over by the dirt pile where big beams of steel arrive
works a daddy pipe layer with his little pipers **FIVE**.

"Lay!" says the daddy. "We lay!" say the five.
So they lay plunk plunk where big beams of steel arrive.

Over by the dirt pile near a stack of brawny bricks
works a mummy cement mixer with her little mixers SIX.

"Spin!" says the mummy. "We spin!" say the six.

So they spin chwurl chwurl near a stack of brawny bricks.

Over by the dirt pile, soaring skyward up to heaven,
works a tall mummy crane with her little cranes **SEVEN**.

"Lift!" says the mummy.
"We lift!" say the seven.

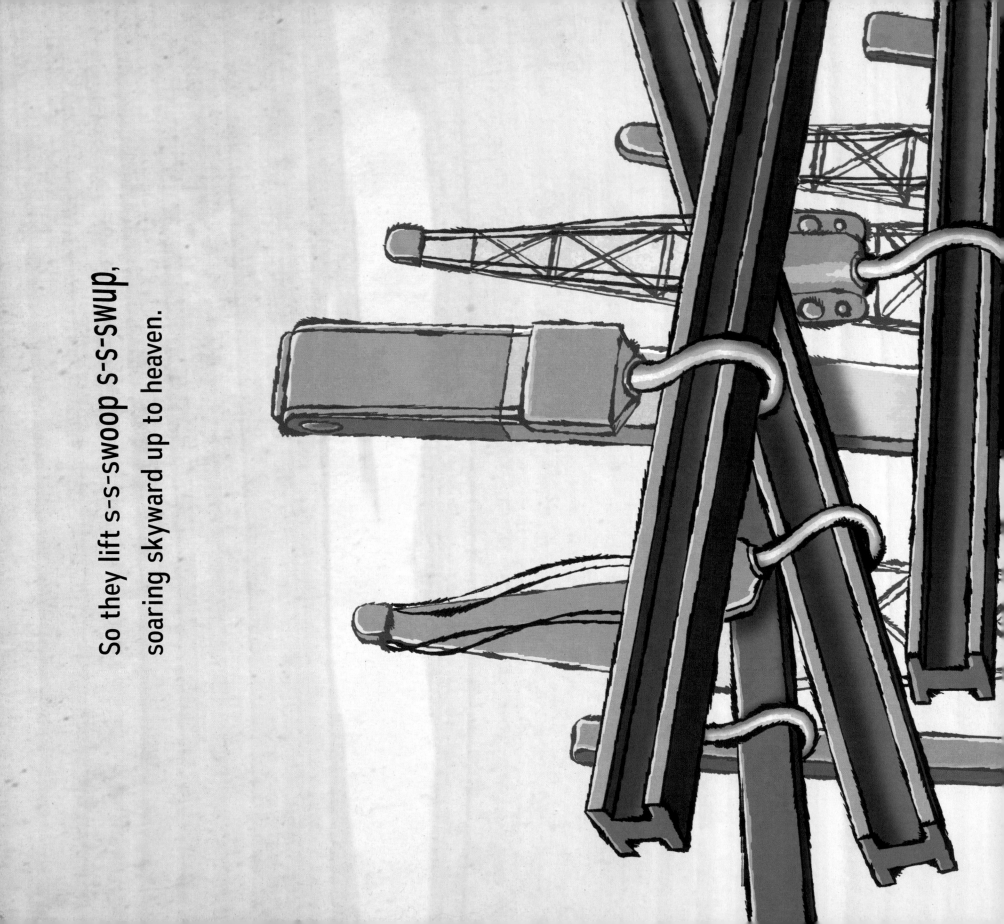

So they lift s-s-swoop s-s-swoop s-s-swup,
soaring skyward up to heaven.

Over by the dirt pile near the wide construction gate
works a strong daddy grader with his little graders **EIGHT**.

"Scrape!" says the daddy. "We scrape!" say the eight.
So they scrape scritch scratch near the wide construction gate.

Over by the dirt pile in a long and hefty line
works a daddy tarmac paver with his little pavers **NINE**.

"Glide!" says the daddy. "We glide!" say the nine.
So they glide **oooz oooz** in a long and hefty line.

Over by the dirt pile, wearing such a toothy grin,
works a mummy steamroller with her little rollers **TEN**.

"Mash!" says the mummy. "We mash!" say the ten.
So they mash *moosh moosh*, wearing such big toothy grins.

Over by the dirt pile
in the sinking summer sun,
those trucks all give a shout —
TOOT! TOOT! —
for their hard work day is done.

Soon it's time to snooze.

They scrubble up, then snuggle in.

All listen to truck lullabies
as lights blink wink and dim.

The moon glows cosy bright
as they whisper, "Nighty night."

Then — they dream about tomorrow at the big construction site. Shhh...